To

From

KAY THOMPSON'S

ELOISE

AT

CHRISTMASTIME

DRAWINGS BY
HILARY KNIGHT

SIMON & SCHUSTER BOOKS FOR YOUNG READERS

SIMON & SCHUSTER BOOKS FOR YOUNG READERS

AN IMPRINT OF SIMON & SCHUSTER CHILDREN'S PUBLISHING DIVISION

1230 AVENUE OF THE AMERICAS

NEW YORK, NEW YORK 10020

COPYRIGHT © 1958 BY KAY THOMPSON

COPYRIGHT © RENEWED 1986 / KAY THOMPSON

NEW ILLUSTRATIONS BY HILARY KNIGHT ON PAGES 12-13, 26, 50-51, 52-53

COPYRIGHT © 1999 BY THE ESTATE OF KAY THOMPSON

FOR MOTHER AND KAY. LOVE, SISTIE.

FOR HENRY, 1941–1989 – H.K.

ALL RIGHTS RESERVED INCLUDING THE RIGHT OF REPRODUCTION IN WHOLE OR IN PART IN ANY FORM.

SIMON & SCHUSTER BOOKS FOR YOUNG READERS IS A TRADEMARK OF SIMON & SCHUSTER.

PRINTED IN THE UNITED STATES OF AMERICA

FIRST EDITION, 1958

FIRST SIMON & SCHUSTER BOOKS FOR YOUNG READERS EDITION, 1999

1 3 5 7 9 10 8 6 4 2

LIBRARY OF CONGRESS CARD CATALOG NUMBER: 58-11869

ISBN 0-689-83039-4

Once there was this little child

You know her I believe

Here's who she is me ELOISE

And it is Christmas Eve

It's Christmas Eve
with a blizzard outside
And four below zero
or more

But inside the Plaza
we're cozy and warm
in our rooms
on the tippy top floor

Ooooooooooooooooooooo!

We're Skipperdee who is my turtle

and Weenie who is my dog

Nanny my mostly companion

and ME

and the blazing

Yuletide log

Our face is absolutely aglow

Then it's dash away jingle
to hear Nanny say
"Do mind the tree my dear
I'd rawther you didn't
come into this closet
I'm hiding the presents
in here"

You can hear Nanny say
"Oh trinkles
my dear
Oh drinkles and sklinkles of fun
It's Christmas
Christmas
Christmas Eve
Oh my
there's a lot to be done"

I agree with her

So I put on my Christmas jingle bells
and jingle around or so
Into this Christmas closet
for my halo of mistletoe

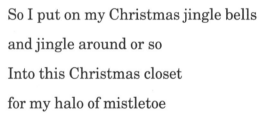

It is absolutely sweet

While Nanny is filling the stockings

I shout out loud and clear

"I must go down

to the lobby

to spread some Christmas cheer"

And Nanny says

"Of course

of course

of course

you must my dear"

Then I jingle out to the elevator

All of the cars are full

to the brim

because of the holiday

God rest ye merry gentlemen

Let nothing you dismay

It is rawther crowded

Fa la la la fa la la lolly ting tingledy here and there. Blow music of trinkles and drinkles of glass it's Christmas everywhere

And you should see the lobby

You absolutely can't get near it

There are all these people

roaming around

Filled with the Christmas spirit

I usually wear a star or so

in case there is this package

that doesn't know where it's going

Fa la la la fa la la lolly ting tingledy here and there. Blow music of trinkles and drinkles of glass there's Christmas everywhere

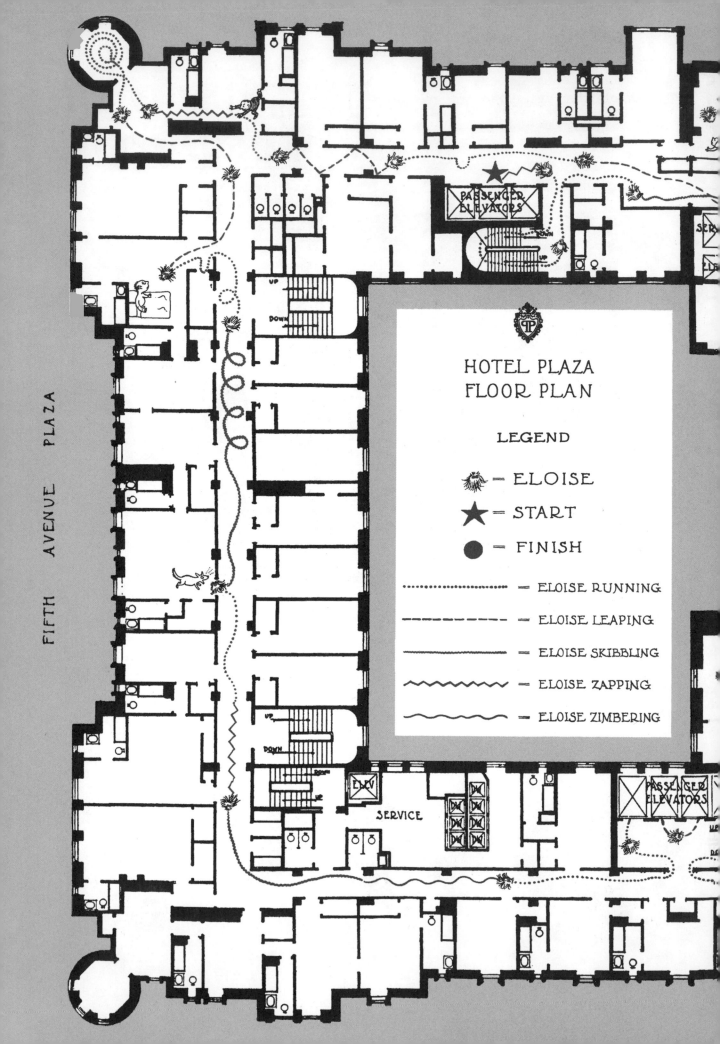

FIFTH AVENUE PLAZA

PASSENGER ELEVATORS

SERVICE

HOTEL PLAZA
FLOOR PLAN

LEGEND

= ELOISE

★ = START

● = FINISH

.... = ELOISE RUNNING

– – – – = ELOISE LEAPING

———— = ELOISE SKIBBLING

〰〰〰 = ELOISE ZAPPING

~~~~~ = ELOISE ZIMBERING

PASSENGER ELEVATORS

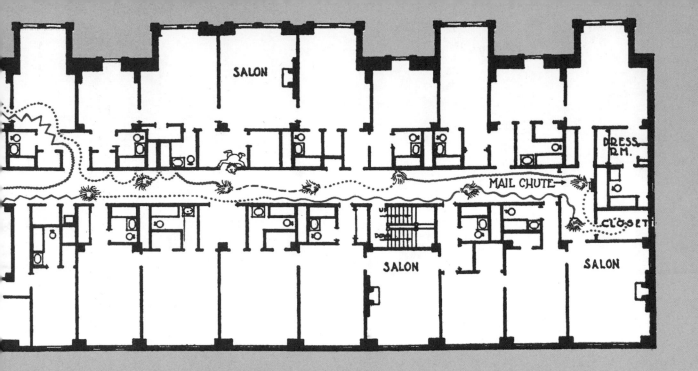

Then it's zippity jingle and dash away ping

Hang holly and berries in all the halls

Tie tassels on all the thermostats and

Write Merry Christmas on all of the walls

I go to as many holiday parties as I possibly can

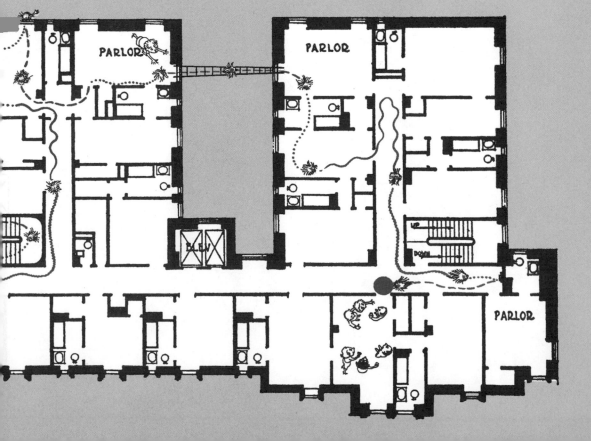

They are rawther festive

Oh zippity jingle and dash away tingle

to shout out loud and clear

Oh come All Ye Faithful

It's me ELOISE Nanny dear

You can hear Nanny say

"Put the peppermint sticks

over there

with the cookies and fruities

and do

oh do

oh do

get on

with all of your Christmas duties

Now

who who who

in the whole wide world

Could be sending American Beauties?"

Oh trinkles oh trinkles sing fa la la lolly ting tingle bells there and here. It's the absolutelyiest busiest time of the year the year the year ping ping

Oh candy the apples
Oh shell the nuts
Oh crackledy crack yum yum
Trink trinkle around the taffy box
Oh yum gulp gulp and yum

Weenie usually helps me
But this year he will not budge
unless he has two of peppermint puffs
and one and a half of fudge

I usually have two of peppermint puffs
and three or four of fudge

Skipperdee dislikes peppermint puffs
and won't even smell the fudge

I have to do quite a bit
of trimming
for it's Christmas Eve tonight
trim trinkles and drinkles
and sklinkles of glass
Trim everything in sight

𝄞 Jingle here jingle there jingle Christmas everywhere

We hang everything
on our Christmas tree
Ornaments big and bright
and all of these
sparkling icicles
and twirling balls of white

I always hang a star on top
With angels in between

Here's how many lights we have—
Thirty-seven and sixteen

I am giving the bellboys earmuffs
The waiters baseball socks
Thomas is getting a vest with a bib
Room service a music box

And for my friend Vincent the barber
this rawther unusual brush
with rawther unusual bristles
that got caught in the Christmas rush

But wrap it oh wrap it oh holly oh Christmas
in tinsel and ribbon and paste
Then stick with a sticker a seal and a card
TO THE BARBER SHOP POSTHASTE

I'm giving Mr. Harris in catering
a pair of woollen gloves
and a piece of fruit cake from Japan
which he absolutely loves

For the 59th Street doorman
a bottle of Guinness Stout
to keep him warm on the inside
when there's a blizzard on the out

And for that darling carriage horse
who stands across the street
a blanket with his initials on it
and a Christmas boiled sweet

I sent a folding Christmas card
to the ducks in Central Park
Skipperdee thought he had captured a bug
but it was only a yuletide spark

The special delivery postman arrived
at absolutely hawlf pawst ten
It was a zippy bag from my mother's lawyer
so I wrapped it back up again

I got a present for Nanny for Nanny for Nanny
but don't tell her
It's a little silver thimble full of
frankincense and myrrh

For Weenie a roastbeef bone deluxe
For Skipperdee raisin milk
I'm giving the valet a beehive of course
made of safety pins and silk

And when my gifts are delivered and wrapped
and put under the tree tree tree
I have to trim this children's one
for Weenie and skipperdee

If anyone remembers
the porter needs suspenders

Sometimes there is so much to do that
I get sort of a headache around the sides and partially under it

Give a Christmas stocking at Christmastime

and here's the thing of it

It doesn't matter if it has a hole or not

put a poinsettia

in it in it

or a nut

if that

doesn't

fit

But you absolutely <u>have</u> to put

a present inside of it of it

Oh trinkles oh trinkles sing fa la la la lolly ring tinkle bells here and there. Blow music of trinkles and drinkles of glass there's Christmas everywhere

Then I must lie down

and smell the pine

and gaze at the Christmas star

Perchance to feel in these piney pine needles

just where

my presents are

For when you are a child of six
it's difficult to know
if you deserve a present or not
at Christmastime
or so

So if no one remembers me
and no presents can I find
I'll know I don't deserve them
It doesn't matter
I don't mind

Fa la la la fa la la la lolly ting tingles of angel hair. Blow music of trinkles and drinkles of glass there's Christmas everywhere

Put a candle in the window

This glistening Christmas light

For a lonely stranger passing by

to come in and out of the night

𝄞 Fa la la la fa la la la lolly ting tingles of angel hair. Blow music of trinkles and drinkles of glass there's Christmas everywhere

My favorite carol

is trinkles and drinkles

and Nanny's absolute choice

is We Three Kings of Orient Are

She has a rawther unusual voice

Whenever we sing

"Oh still the night

'Ere lo 'ere lo

Comes o'er"

Emily and Weenie and

Skipperdee shout

Encore Encore Encore

Then we all shout bravo

And it's zippety jingle and dashaway ping ting tingles of angel hair. Blow music of trinkles and drinkles of glass there's Christmas everywhere

I'm rawther fond of caroling

Fa la on every floor

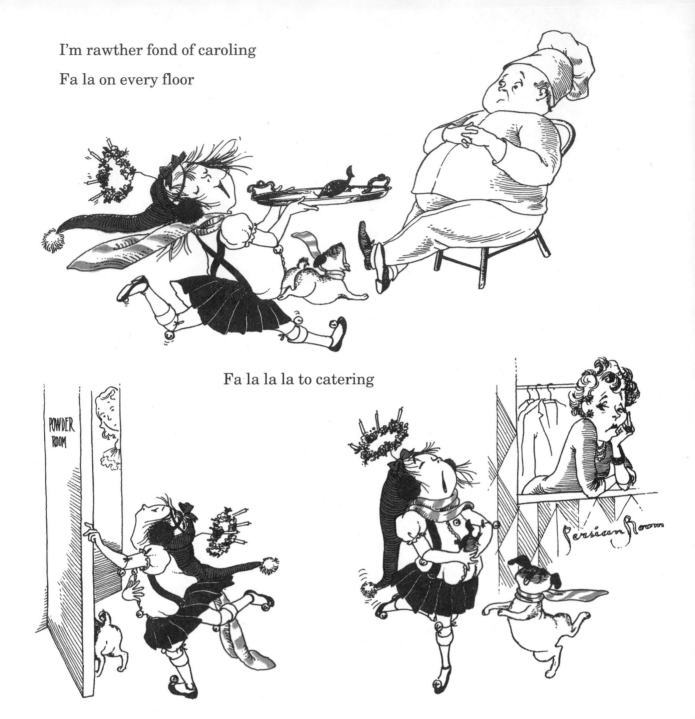

Fa la la la to catering

Fa la from door to door

𝄞 Fa la la la fa la la lolly ting tingles of angel hair. Blow music of trinkles and drinkles of glass there's Christmas everywhere

We sang Noel for 506

Silent Night for 507

We didn't sing for 509

at the request of 511

But ho ho ho and jiggeldy ping

We were not dismayed

We skibbled into the exit sign

and sang

 Oh trinkles oh drinkles fa la fa lo

for Lily

the nightmaid

Skipperdee lost a tooth

singing Good King Wenceslaus

But we found it behind

this azalea plant

hiding under this moss

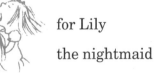

My mother called
long distance
from the Mediterranean
I believe
We talked for an hour and
charged it
like we did last Christmas Eve

She was sunburned on her legs
and sent me this absolutely
sweet cartwheel hat
with these earpuffs on it

I think it looks absolutely darling on me

Emily wasn't feeling well
It's rawther sad to mention
Nanny said "Oh pooh pooh pooh
it's Christmas indigestion"

But she looked like she had a fever or so
especially around the face
So I put this Christmas basket
out on the flagpole
for her
just in case

I usually walk around quite a bit or so thinking of a way to stay up hawlf the night

Oh trinkles oh trinkles sing fa la la la lolly ring tinkle bells here and there. Blow music of trinkles and drinkles of glass there's Christmas everywhere

Then Nanny stretched and yawned out loud
and cheerily inquired
"What <u>are</u> we doing
up up up
when we're so tired tired tired?"

"Let's jingle to bed

Now there's a girl

Let's have no tears of sorrow

Let's close our eyes

and sleep sleep sleep

so we can carry on tomorrow"

I always hang a two legged Christmas stocking just in case

Some of us were rawther tired

Then some of us sort of closed some of our eyes
to have this Christmas dream

of some steaming hot plum pudding

with extra cream cream cream

Of reindeers with sunglasses on
ice-skating on the stars
with mittens on their antlers
and mufflers made in Mars

And Santa chuckled and said "Dash on to the Plaza my lovely boys
We'll have Christmas punch with Nanny and give Eloise her toys"

I thought he looked terribly well

And when we awakened
he'd come and gone
and in all of this midnight and dark
we could see these reindeers zimbering
through the trees in Central Park

We could even see this tail-light
on Santa Claus' sleigh

and Emily had a baby pigeon
on absolutely Christmas day

Of course she named it Raphael,
because it was born in this big hotel

"Bleh-ess you dear Emily"
Nanny then said
"Now what time can it possibly be?"
We said
"It's absolutely Christmas
and time to sklinkle off to the tree"
"Of course" she yawned "of course of course
Sing trinkles and follow me"

And we did

And we laughed and dawnced in our Christmas barefeet ting ting to the Christmas tree

Then oh oh oh absolutely oh oh

Oh trinkles and sklinkles of glee

Oh look oh look oh <u>will</u> you look

at the presents under the tree

And in all of this

everly Christmas excitement

we could hardly wait to see

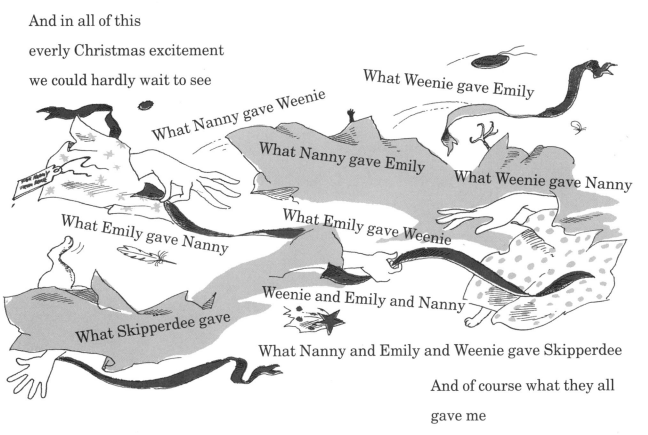

What Nanny gave Weenie

What Weenie gave Emily

What Nanny gave Emily

What Weenie gave Nanny

What Emily gave Weenie

What Emily gave Nanny

Weenie and Emily and Nanny

What Skipperdee gave

What Nanny and Emily and Weenie gave Skipperdee

And of course what they all

gave me

And everyone shouted and yelled oh oh oh

and unwrapped this Christmas surprise

And some of us couldn't believe what

we saw

with some of our Christmas eyes

Weenie was digging
as he usually does
around this Christmas tree
and under this light
to the left of this bough
we found this present for me

And this dear little angel
with snow on her head
Said
"What can this possibly be?"

Then Nanny said
"Little Miss Christmas
Miss Christmas
Miss Christmas
that one is from me"
"Oh Nanny how darling!
What is it?" I said
She said
"Open it up and see"

And there it was
and it sparkled at me
A diamond necklace of trinkles and glue
"Oh trinkles" I said
"Nanny dear I love you
I absolutely do"

Here is who my absolutely best friend
in this whole wide world is
Nanny

Then it's up and it's oh
to the telephone go
"Hello there Room Service Dear
Send Christmas breakfast
on Christmas trays
to these four Christmas children
up here

"And if you'd like
to nibble on something
like some Christmas
cinnamon trees
Simply tell the chef
to bake some at once
and charge it to me
ELOISE"

They're absolutely delicious

It's absolutely Christmas
so come to the top floor please
come all of my friends where ever you are
For a trinkle with
ME
ELOISE

Jingle

Jingle

Jingle

here

Jingle

there

Jingle

Christmas

everywhere

Jingle

Jingle

Jingle

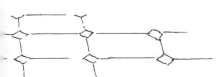

Oooooooooooooooooooooooo! I absolutely love Christmas